AF348306

Jhanvi Latheesh

Jhanvi Latheesh is born in Kannur, Kerala and settled in Dubai. She started her journey with books at the age of 5 which grew along with her. Her love for reading inspired her in writing stories on her own. She is studying in grade 5. Apart from reading, Jhanvi is also interested in dancing and drawing. She express her gratitude saying Thank you universe for making this happen my First book "Wondrous Adventures".

English Language
Wondrous Adventures
(Stories)
by
Jhanvi Latheesh

♦

Published in September 2024
by Kairali Books Private Limited
Thalikkavu Road, Kannur.
Ph : 0497-2761200
E-Mail : kairalibooksknr@gmail.com

♦

Illustrations & Cover Design
Watermelon

♦

© All rights reserved
No part of this publication may be reproduced, stored in or
introduced into a retrieval system, or transmitted, in any form, or
by any means, electronic, mechanical, photocopying, recording or
otherwise without the prior written permission of the publisher.

77/24-25/Sl.No.1644/200/NS.18.6
ISBN 978-93-5973-820-8

Wondrous Adventures

Jhanvi Latheesh

Kairali Books

WONDROUS ADVENTURES

The book "WONDROUS ADVENTURES"- stories for children is a collection of funny and captivating short stories written especially for children aged 5 to 10. In this book young readers will find 12 exciting stories that will stimulate and spark their imagination.

The stories are full of exciting characters and places that will take children on a journey through their imagination. Each story has a unique message that will inspire readers to have their own adventures and pursue their dreams.

The first story is about a little boy named Max who discovers a magical door that leads him to another world. In another story, readers meet a talking squirrel named Sammy who has lost his nut and needs help finding it.

There are stories about astronauts, pirates, bears, princesses and many other fascinating characters. Each story is written in a way that keeps children interested and encourages them to keep reading.

This book is divided into short, easy to digest chapters that are perfect for reading aloud before bedtime or for independent reading. The lively language and colorful illustrations also make the book appealing to visual learners.

"Wondrous Adventures-Stories for kids" is a book that takes children on an exciting journey through their imagination while teaching them valuable lessons about friendship, cohesion and following their dreams.

JHANVI LATHEESH

CONTENTS

1

Max and the magic door

Max was a curious boy who was always looking for new adventures. One day he discovered an old shed in his garden that he had never noticed before. When he got closer, he discovered a small door that he had never seen before. Without hesitation, he opened the door and stepped through.

What Max found on the other side was beyond his wildest dreams. A beautiful landscape full of colors and lights stretched out before him. A small stream meandered through the grass and majestic mountains rose into the sky on the horizon.

Max could hardly believe his eyes and began to explore the area. He discovered animals he had never seen before and plants as tall as trees. He kept walking and finally discovered a group of creatures that looked like humans, but were much smaller.

They called themselves "The shimmering ones" and greeted Max in a friendly manner. They led him to their village where he discovered many wondrous things. There were flying butterflies and sparkling gems floating in the air. It was a magical world full of wonders. Max spent many

happy days in the world behind the doors and learned a lot from the shimmering ones.

But one day he remembered that he had to go back home. He knew his family was worried and he had to return. When he had returned to the door, he found it locked. He did not know how to return. But the shimmering ones had an idea. They gave him a magic stone that would take him back to his own world.

Max took the stone and closed his eyes. When he opened them again, he was back in his garden. The door and the shed were gone. Max looked around and smiled. He knew that he had an incredible adventure and that he could always return to visit his friends in the world beyond the door.

And so it was that Max learned a valuable lesson : that the world is full of wonders and that adventures are waiting for us everywhere .You just have to keep your eyes open and have the courage to step through the door.

2

Pieps learns to fly

Pieps was a little sparrow who lived in a cozy nest in a tree high up in the clouds. He was curious and always wanted to see more of the world. Every day he saw another birds flying through the air and admired their freedom and ability to fly anywhere.

One day, Pieps decided it was time to spread his wings and explore the world. He looked out of the nest and saw the sky in all its color and beauty .He knew he could fly because, after all, he had wings, but he had never tried to really fly before.

So Pieps jumped off the branch with excitement and fluttered his wings, but he quickly fell to the ground. He had no idea what he had done wrong and was sad that he could not fly. At that moment, a wise old bird named Grandpa came by. Grandpa had travelled around the world many times and knew many stories. He had seen many little birds like Pieps who had hurt themselves because they thought they could just fly without ever learning how.

Grandpa asked Pieps what had happened, and when he heard the story, he explained to him that just having wings

is not enough to be able to fly. Flying requires practice and training. Pieps was sad, but Grandpa offered to train him and show him how to fly. Pieps was excited about the idea, although he was also a little scared. But he knew he wanted to learn so he could fly freely in the air.

Grandpa showed Pieps how to use the wings properly and how to stay in the air. He also showed Pieps how to use thermals to fly higher and how to land gently. Pieps watched Grandpa Closely and tried to learn everything he could.

Although Pieps often had a hard time and fell to the ground every now and then he didn't give up. He was determined to learn how to fly. Day after day he practiced and got better and better. One day, the time had finally come: Pieps could fly! He was so happy and proud of himself .He flew through the air and discovered a new world full of wonders and adventures.

However, Pieps learned much more from his journey. He learned that sometimes things take time and practice to learn. He also learned that it's okay to make mistakes as long as you learn from them and move on. And most importantly, he learned that he can always ask someone for help if he can't do something on his own.

3

Max and the treasure of the jungle

Max was a bright boy who was always up for adventures. One day he heard about an old treasure that was supposed to be hidden somewhere deep in the jungle. Max was exited and decided to find the treasure.

He started to research everything about the treasure and got himself a map. The map was full of riddles and clues that needed to be deciphered. Max was not discouraged and set off into the jungle.

He fought his way through dense forests, difficult rivers and steep mountains. It was a difficult journey, but Max did not give up. Finally he reached the place where the treasure was supposed to be hidden.

But when he got there, he found only an empty treasure chest. He was disappointed, but he didn't give up. He knew there was more to discover.

As he went deeper into the jungle, he found a hidden door in an old ruin. He opened the door and discovered a secret chamber full of treasures! It was breathtaking sight. Gold, diamonds and precious stones were scattered everywhere.

Max was thrilled and felt incredibly happy. But as he took a step closer, he suddenly heard a loud growl. He turned

around and saw a huge tiger standing right in front of him. The tiger had apparently wanted to defend its territory.

Max was panicked and didn't know what to do. He had never seen a tiger so close. However, he was aware that he could not just run away. He stood still and tried to remain calm. The tiger stared at him and seemed to be preparing to attack.

But suddenly Max heard another sound. It was the sound of a group of elephants. The elephants came closer and closer and the tiger became more and more nervous. Finally, he gave up and disappeared into the jungle.

Max was relieved and grateful for the elephants. He spent some more time exploring the treasures and then returned home full of joy. He knew he had an incredible experience and that he would always remember the elephants who had saved him. And so it was that, Max learned a valuable lesson: that you have to set out to have adventures, and that you never know what to expect. But most importantly, there was always friends and helpers to stand by us in difficult times.

4

Sammy's search for the lost nut

Sammy was a little squirrel with shiny red fur and big, curious eyes. He loved to run through the forest, climb trees and collect nuts. One day, however, while he was out looking for nuts, something terrible happened: Sammy lost his favorite nuts!

He had been saving the nut for weeks and was very proud of it. It was the biggest and the tastiest nut he had ever found. But when he tripped over a tree root, it fell out of his hand and rolled down the hill where it disappeared into the bushes.

Sammy tried to find the nut, but it was futile. The sun was setting, and he decide to go home and continue searching the next day. But the next day he still could not find the nut. He asked all the animals in the forest if they had seen his nut, but no one had found it.

Discouraged and sad, Sammy returned to his tree house. He just couldn't stop thinking about his lost nut. It was as if a part of him was missing. But then an idea came to him: he would put together a search party and ask all the animals in the forest for help.

Sammy would go to every animal in the forest and ask for help in finding his nut. The first one he met was Timmy,

a smart raccoon. Timmy told him that he had a sense of smell like a bloodhound and would help him find the nut. Together they searched the forest, sniffing every bush and tree and even reaching into molehills, but the nut was nowhere to be found.

Then Sammy met Lilly, a nimble lizard. She told him that she was good at looking for and finding holes. Together they searched all the holes in the forest, but again the nut was nowhere to be found.

Sammy did not give up, however. He knew he needed help, so he kept asking all the animals in the forest if they could help him. Finally, he met an old squirrel named Grandpa Oak. Grandpa Oak was wise and had lot of experience. He told Sammy not to look for the nut, but that the nut would find him when he least expected it.

Sammy was confused, but he decided to follow the old squirrel's advice. He stopped looking for the nut and spent his days playing and romping in the forest with his friends.

One day, while Sammy was playing tag with his friends, he heard a soft giggle behind him. He turned around and saw his nut roll out of a bush and come to a stop at his feet. He could hardly believe his eyes, but he knew that Grandpa Oak was right: the nut had found him when he least expected it.

Sammy could hardly believe his luck. He has found his nut again! He picked it up and looked at it with shining eyes. The nut was a little scratched and has a few bumps, but to Sammy it was still the most beautiful nut in the world.

He thanked his friends for helping him find the nut, even if they didn't find it right away. Without their support, he would not have stopped looking for it and would never have found his nut. Full of joy, Sammy ran back to his tree house to put his nut in a safe place. He would now keep it forever and take good care of it. And when he went looking for nuts in the future, he would be even more careful so that something like this would never happen to him again.

The other animals in the forest were thrilled that Sammy had found his nut again. They were proud of their cooperation and friendship with Sammy. From that day on, they played together even more often and helped each other whenever they could.

Sammy had learned that sometimes it's better to stop looking for something and instead just enjoy life and focus on other things. Because sometimes you find what you're looking for when you least expect it.

5

A girl and her squirrel friend

Once upon a time there was a little girl named Lena. Lena loved being outside in nature and watching animals. One day, in a nearby forest, she discovered a little squirrel lying helplessly on the ground. Lena rushed to it and saw that it was injured.

Lena had a big heart and couldn't just leave the little squirrel alone. She decided to take it home and take care of it until it was well again. She named the squirrel Sammy and built him a cozy nest in a basket where he could sleep.

Lena regularly fed Sammy nuts and fruits and washed him when he was dirty. She also played with him often and loved to watch him bounce around and dash about the room. Lena was happy that she could help Sammy and that he was her new best friend.

One day when Lena was feeding Sammy, she noticed that he was still not quite well. His eyes were red and he was breathing heavily. Lena knew she had to do something to help him before it was too late. She decided to take Sammy to the vet.

When they arrived at the vet, Sammy was immediately examined. The vet found that Sammy was suffering from a

severe cold and eye infection. He gave Lena some medication and instructions on how to take care for Sammy to get him better.

Lena followed the vet's instructions closely and made sure Sammy received all the medications and an adequate rest. After a few days, Lena noticed that Sammy was feeling better. His eyes was no longer red and he was breathing much easier.

One day Lena asked Sammy if he wanted to go back to the forest where he belonged. Sammy hesitated because he didn't want to leave Lena, but Lena assured him that he would always be a part of her family and that she would visit him whenever she could.

So Lena took Sammy back to the forest and said goodbye to him. Sammy walked towards a tree and looked back at Lena as if to thank her. Lena waved at him and smiled when she saw how happy Sammy looked.

Lena was sad that Sammy was gone, but she was also proud of herself for helping him get better and go back to the wild. She knew that she would meet many more animals in need, and that she would always be there to help them. And so Lena became a true animal lover and spent many happy days watching and caring for animals. She knew that she has a special gift to understand and help the animals. And that made her a happy girl.

6

A bear friendship

Once upon a time there was a little boy named Max who lived in a small village in the mountains. Max loved being out in the nature and having adventures. One day he decided to climb the highest mountain in the village to enjoy a breathtaking view from the top.

Max started his journey early in the morning and took only the bare necessities with him. He had a water bottle, a flashlight, some snacks and a map of the area. The sun shone brightly in the sky and the birds chirped happily as he marched off.

The trail was steep and strenuous, but Max was not discouraged. He was a brave boy and was determined to reach the top. After a few hours of hiking, he finally reached the highest point of the mountain. He was out of breath, but his joy at the breathtaking view he had was indescribable.

He could see the whole village from above and even the neighboring villages in the distance. The landscape was simply unbelievably beautiful. Max decide to take a break and enjoy his snacks while enjoying the view.

As he rested, he suddenly heard a strange noise. It sounded like scratching and crackling. Max stood up and looked around .To his surprise, he saw a small bear moving out of a bush and looking up at him.

Max was startled at first, but the bear looked so cute that he quickly calmed down. The bear was small and brown and seemed very curious about Max. He came closer and sniffed Max's backpack.

Max smiled and decided to feed the bear. He took some snacks out of his backpack and offered them to the bear. The bear sniffed the snacks and started eating them. Max thought it was funny how the bear held the snacks with his little paws and shoved them into his mouth.

They sat there together for a while, enjoying the view and the sun. The bear seemed to have found Max as a new friend and didn't want to leave. Max knew he couldn't take the bear with him and decided to help him go back into the forest.

He carefully grabbed the bear and carried it down the mountain. The bear seemed to trust Max and even lay down in his arms when he got tired. Max knew he couldn't keep the bear with him forever and decided to take him back to the forest once he recovered.

When they reached the forest, Max looked for a comfortable place for the bear to rest and recover. He found a small cave that was perfect for the bear. Max gathered some branches and leaves and made a cozy bed for the bear in the cave. The bear immediately curled up and slept soundly. Max stayed with him for a while longer to make

sure he was okay.

When it was time to go back to the village, Max said goodbye to the bear and promised to visit him again soon. The bear seemed to understand him and gave him a sad look as Max left. On the way home, Max was still full of energy and excitement. He couldn't wait to tell his parents and friends about his adventure. When he returned to the village, he told everyone about the bear he had met on the mountain. Everyone was amazed and asked him how he had managed to tame a wild bear.

Max felt great and proud of himself for helping the bear. He decided to return and visit him again as soon as he could. He wanted to make sure the bear was safe and healthy. Over the next few weeks, Max visited the bear regularly, bringing him food and water. The bear seemed to have grown accustomed to Max and waited for him every time he came. Max and the bear spent a lot of time together exploring the forest and the mountains.

One day, Max decided it was time to say goodbye to the bear. He knew that the bear would soon return to the wild and that it was time to let him go. Max promised to always keep him in his heart and visit him in his thoughts.

When he got back to the village, Max told everyone about his adventure with the bear and how he had helped him. The people in the village were so impressed with his story that they decided to hold a small ceremony for him to honor his bravery.

Max was touched and grateful for the support and recognition of his friends and neighbors. He knew that he had an unforgettable experience and that he would always be proud of having helped the bear. And so ends the story of Max and the bear. A story of friendship and adventure that shows that sometimes the most unexpected encounters can lead to the greatest experiences.

7

Buddy, the rescued bird
-a story about friendship and help

Once upon a time there was a little boy named Tim who loved to play outside. One day, when he was in the playground, he noticed a little bird stuck in a tree. The bird has gotten caught in a branch and couldn't get free.

Tim had a big heart and decided to help the bird. He called his friends and they all came together to free the bird. They tried to move the branch carefully, but the bird was too stuck. They didn't know what to do.

But then Tim had an idea. He had heard that his neighbor, Mrs. Schmidt, had a good idea when it came to helping animals. Tim ran home and asked his mother to take him to Frau Schmidt. Mrs. Schmidt was an old women who loved all animals. She had a large collection of animal books and knew how to help animals in need. Tim explained the situation with the bird and asked for her help.

Mrs. Schmidt took her things and went to the playground with Tim and his friends. She examined the birds and found that it was not injured, but was indeed stuck. She got some tools out of her bag and carefully began to remove the branch.

After a few minutes, they had successfully removed the branch and the bird flew away. Tim and his friends were so happy that they had saved the bird. They thanked Mrs. Schmidt and went home happy.

The next day, Tim was at the playground and saw that the bird had returned .The bird flew up to Tim and sat on his shoulder. Tim knew that the bird was thanking him for saving him. From that day on, the bird was always near Tim when he was on the playground. Tim and his friends had made a new friend and they named the bird "Buddy". They made sure Buddy always had enough food and water and played with him often. Tim and his friends had learned how important it is to help animals in need. They had also learned that there is always someone who can help if you just ask. They were proud to have rescued Buddy and promised to always look out for him. And so, all summer long, Tim, his friends and Buddy played on the playground and had a wonderful time together.

8

Max and the mouse

Once upon a time there was a little boy named Max. Max was a curious boy who was always looking for adventure. One day, while Max was playing in his garden, he heard a noise coming from the bushes. Curious as he was, he looked to see what it could be.

To his surprise, he found a little mouse lost in the bushes. The mouse was trembling with fear and didn't seem to be moving. Max knew he had to help. He carefully took the mouse in the palm of his hand and carried it into the house.

Once in the kitchen, Max grabbed a bowl and filled it with a few crumbs from his breakfast sandwich. The little mouse seemed to recover and began nibbling the crumbs. Max was so glad that he had rescued the mouse. He decided to give her a new home. He built a little house out of an old shoebox, put some scraps of cloth inside and carefully placed the mouse inside.

The mouse seemed comfortable in its new home and began to run around and explore. Max was so happy to be able to give the little mouse a new life. In the days and weeks that followed, Max visited the mouse in her home every

day. He brought her food and water and spent hours keeping her company. The mouse seemed to become more and more attached to Max and became his loyal friend.

One day when Max visited the mouse, he noticed that she was no longer alone. The little mouse had given birth to five little baby mice. Max was so happy and excited that he welcomed the little mice with open arms.

Over the next few weeks, Max lovingly cared for the mouse and her babies. He gave them food and water and played with them. The little baby mice grew quickly and began to explore. One day, max decided it was time to release the mice into the wild. He packed the shoebox and took it to the garden. Carefully, he opened the box and released the mice. The mice ran and played around the garden and seemed happier than ever. Max was so happy that he was able to help the little mouse and her babies start a new life in freedom. From that day on, Max regularly visited the mice in the garden and spent hours keeping them company. He was happy that he could help them, and the mice were happy to have a friend like Max.

9

Tim and the adventure as a pirate

Once upon a time there was a little boy named Tim who dreamed of being a pirate. Every time he passed by the harbor, he watched the big sailing ships and imagined what it would be like to sail the high seas and have adventures.

One day, while Tim was playing at the harbor, he heard a loud roar and saw a huge ship enter the harbor. It was the ship of the infamous pirate captain Blackbeard. Tim could hardly contain his excitement and decided to sneak onto the ship to become a real pirate.

Once he was on board the ship, he discovered that it was full of pirates who all looked very intimidating .Tim hid in an empty barrel and hoped that no one would find him. But it wasn't long before one of the pirates spotted him,

The pirate, a tall man with a beard and an eye patch, asked Tim what he was doing on the ship. Tim told him that he wanted to be a pirate and asked if he could come and stay on the ship. The pirate named Long John took Tim under his wing and taught him everything he needed to know about being a pirate. Tim learned how to sail, how to fight and how to find treasure. He had a great time on the ship and

enjoyed the adventure he was given.

One day the crew discovered a treasure map that showed the way to a hidden treasure. The crew decided to go on a treasure hunt, and Tim was excited to finally find a real treasure. They sailed the high seas and fought other pirates to find the treasure. After many days and nights at sea, they finally discovered a small island where the treasure was located.

The crew went ashore and began to search for the treasure. Tim was excited and helped with the search until he finally found the treasure. It was a box full of gold coins and jewels. The crew celebrated and Tim was made an official member of the pirate crew. They sailed back to the harbor, where Tim was made an official member of the pirate crew. They sailed back to the harbor, where Tim decided to continue his adventures as a pirate and one day became a captain himself.

From that day on, Tim knew that he could accomplish anything he set mind to as long as he believed in himself and worked hard. And he also knew that there was nothing more exciting than the life of a Pirate.

10

Lena in Space

Once upon a time, there was a little girl named Lena who had dreamed of becoming an astronaut for as long as she could remember. She was fascinated by stories about space travel and distant planets and couldn't wait to go into space herself.

One day, Lena had the opportunity to see a real rocket. She was standing in front of the window, staring at the majestic vehicle, when suddenly a man in an astronaut suit stepped out of the door. "Wow", Lena thought." That's a real astronaut!"

The astronaut saw the girl standing and gave her a friendly wave. Lena waved back and smiled. "I'm Jim," the astronaut said. "I'm going into space today. Would you like to come along?" Lena could hardly believe it. "Really? Can I really go to space with you?" Jim nodded. "But you'll have to be quick. The rocket takes off in ten minutes!"

Lena ran as fast as she could to the door and followed Jim into the rocket. She sat in a seat and fastened her seat belt while Jim took care of the final preparations.

Then Lena heard the roar of the engines and felt the rocket

slowly rise from the earth. She pressed her nose against the window and watched the landscape get smaller and smaller. Finally, they were high enough to see the curvature of the Earth. "This is incredible", Lena whispered.

Jim smiled, "Yes, it's an incredible feeling. But we have to keep flying if we want to reach our destination." They flew through space, passing stars and planets, until finally they saw a small, blue planet in the distance.

"This is the planet we want to explore, "Jim said, "Are you ready?" Lena nodded excitedly. Together they boarded the lander and touched down on the planet. They disembarked and explored the landscape, collecting samples and taking photos. When the time came to return to earth, they flew in their rocket and launched back into space. Lena looked around and thought, "One day I'm going to be a real astronaut."

And who knows? Maybe one day she would actually explore the stars and have her own adventures in space.

11

Tim and Emily: Siblings stick together

Once upon a time there was a family with three children: an older brother named Tim, a younger sister named Emily, and a baby named Lily. Tim and Emily were very different, but they still loved each other very much.

Tim was always very athletic and loved being outside and playing with friends. Emily, on the other hand, was more introverted and spent her time painting or reading. But when Tim and Emily were together, they always had a lot of fun.

One day, the family decided to go to an amusement park. Tim and Emily were so excited that they could hardly sleep. When they arrived, they immediately rushed into the park to try out the many rides and attractions.

Tim and Emily rode the roller coaster, carousel and many other rides together. They laughed and screamed with joy and enjoyed every minute.

But then something terrible happened. While waiting in line for the next ride, they noticed that Lily was gone. The family looked everywhere for the baby, but she was nowhere to be found. Tim and Emily were distraught. They had never been so scared. They knew they had to find the baby before

something bad happen.

So they went to the park and looked everywhere for the baby. They searched all the attractions they had visited and asked the staff for help. But no one had seen Lily.

The sun was starting to set and the park was beginning to empty. Tim and Emily were tired and exhausted, but they didn't give up. They decided to go to the back of the park, where they had not yet looked.

There they finally found Lily in her stroller. She had been sound asleep and obviously hadn't gone far.

Tim and Emily were relieved and hugged the baby tightly. They returned to their parents, who were relieved and happy to hold their missing daughter in their arms again. The family went home, but Tim and Emily had grown even closer because of this experience. They now knew that they could always rely on each other and that as siblings they had a strong bond that could never be broken.

12

Pip and the lost Rainbow

Pip wasn't like the other clouds. Oh, he was fluffy and white and loved to drift across the sky, but he had a secret. A magical secret. Pip could make rainbows.

Not just any rainbows, mind you. Pip's rainbows shimmered with every color imaginable, from fiery reds and oranges to calming blues and purples. And when sunlight danced through his rainbows, it wasn't just pretty to look at. It made everyone who saw it feel happy, hopeful, and full of joy.

Pip loved sharing his rainbows with the world. He'd puff himself up, gather every drop of sun kissed rain he could find, and then……whoosh! A magnificent rainbow would burst forth, arching across the sky like a giant smile.

Birds would chirp louder, flowers would bloom brighter, and even grumpy old Mr. Thundercloud would crack a smile. Pip's rainbows were pure magic.

But one day, something strange happened. Pip was creating a rainbow over a field of sunflowers when he noticed the colors weren't as vibrant as usual. The reds seemed dull, the blues faded. Pip tried again, puffing harder and gathering more rain, but the rainbow remained weak and pale.

Worried, Pip floated over to his wise friend, Granny cumulus. Granny cumulus had been a cloud for ages and she knew everything there was to know about the sky.

"Granny," Pip said, his voice trembling," my rainbows are losing their magic. What's happening?"

Granny cumulus stroked her fluffy beard thoughtfully. "This is no ordinary fading, Pip "she said. "I fear someone has stolen the rainbow's magic."

Pip gasped "stolen? But who would do such a thing?"

"There is a dark sorcerer named Nimbus, "Granny cumulus explained. "He envies the joy your rainbows bring and wants to use their magic for his own wicked purposes."

Pip felt a shiver run through his fluffy form. Nimbus was known throughout the sky for his gloomy demeanor and his love of storms. He despised happiness and wanted to cover the world in darkness.

"But what can I do?" Pip asked, feeling small and helpless.

Granny Cumulus smiled gently. "You are not helpless, Pip. You are the rainbow maker. You must find Nimbus and reclaim the stolen magic."

Pip took a deep breath, his heart pounding. He knew this would be a dangerous journey, but he couldn't let Nimbus get away with stealing the rainbow's magic.

With a determined puff, Pip set off on his quest, following the faint trail of the fading rainbow. He didn't know where it would lead him, but he knew he had to try. The world needed his rainbows, and Pip was determined to bring them back.

Pip followed the faint trail of the fading rainbow, his heart

pounding with a mix of determination and fear. The once-vibrant colors were barely a whisper now, leading him towards a dark and ominous part of the sky he'd never dared venture into before.

A s he floated closer, the air grew heavy and cold. The cheerful chirping of birds was replaced by the eerie creaking of thunder. Pip shivered, not from the cold, but from a growing sense of unease.

Suddenly, a bolt of lightning flashed across the sky, illuminating a towering, jagged peak shrouded in darkness. Pip realized this must be Nimbus's lair. Gathering his courage, he floated towards the peak, his tiny form dwarfed by its imposing presence.

The closer he got, the more treacherous the journey became. Jagged rocks jutted out from the peak, threatening to tear his fluffy form. Dark clouds swirled around him, whispering warnings of the dangers ahead.

But Pip pressed on, his determination fueled by the thought of the fading rainbow. He dodged lightning bolts, navigated through swirling winds and even braved a hailstorm, his small body battered but unbroken.

Finally, he reached a hidden cave, its entrance guarded by a swirling vortex of dark clouds. Pip took a deep breath and plunged into the vortex, bracing himself for whatever lay ahead.

The cave was even darker and colder than Pip had imagined. Eerie shadows danced on the walls, and the air crackled with an unsettling energy. But then, in the center of the cave, Pip saw it: the stolen rainbow.

It hung limply from the ceiling, its colors barely visible

in the dim light. Pip's heart ached at the sight. He knew he had to act quickly.

Just as he was about to approach the rainbow, a booming voice echoed through the cave. "Well, well, what have we here? A little cloud who thinks he can defy Nimbus?"

Pip whirled around to see a tall, imposing figure emerge from the shadows. Nimbus was even more intimidating in person, with his dark robes and piercing eyes.

"I've come for the rainbow, Nimbus," Pip declared, his voice surprisingly steady. "You have no right to steal its magic."

Nimbus let out a booming laugh. "Magic? You call that pathetic display of colors magic? It's nothing compared to the power of darkness".

Pip refused to be intimidated. "Your darkness cannot extinguish the light of hope that the rainbows brings," he said. "I will not let you steal that from the world."

Nimbus sneered. "We'll see about that, little cloud. You'll have to get past me first."

And with that, Nimbus raised his arms, and the cave filled with swirling shadows. The temperature plummeted, and icy winds whipped around Pip, trying to extinguish his spirit.

But Pip would not be deterred. He closed his eyes, focusing on the memory of the vibrant rainbow and the joy it brought to the world. He puffed himself up, gathering every ounce of strength he could muster.

Then, with a mighty burst, Pip unleashed his own magic. A brilliant beam of light shot from his fluffy form, cutting through the darkness like a beacon of hope. The shadows recoiled, and the Nimbus stumbles back, his eyes wide with surprise.

Pip pressed his advantage, his light growing brighter and stronger with very passing moment. He knew he couldn't defeat Nimbus with brute force, but he could use his rainbow magic to break the sorcerer's hold on the stolen rainbow.

As the light intensified, the stolen rainbow began to stir. Its colors flickered, then slowly started to regain their vibrancy. Nimbus roared in frustration, but his power was waning.

With one final surge of light, Pip shattered the darkness that held the rainbow captive. The cave filled with a blinding radiance as the rainbow burst forth in all its glory, its colors shimmering with renewed energy.

Nimbus, weakened and defeated, vanished into the shadows. Pip watched him go, feeling a wave of relief wash over him. He had done it. He had saved the rainbow and it's magic.

With a gentle touch, Pip guided the rainbow out of the cave and into the sky. As its vibrant colors filled the world once more, Pip felt a surge of joy and pride. He had faced his fears, overcome great challenges, and ultimately triumphed over darkness.

And as he watched the rainbow bring smiles to the faces of everyone below, Pip knew that his journey had only just begun. There were more rainbows to create, more magic to share, and more adventures to be had. For Pip, the little cloud with big heart, the sky was the limit.

www.ingramcontent.com/pod-product-compliance
Lightning Source LLC
LaVergne TN
LVHW041800190726
843493LV00008B/2717